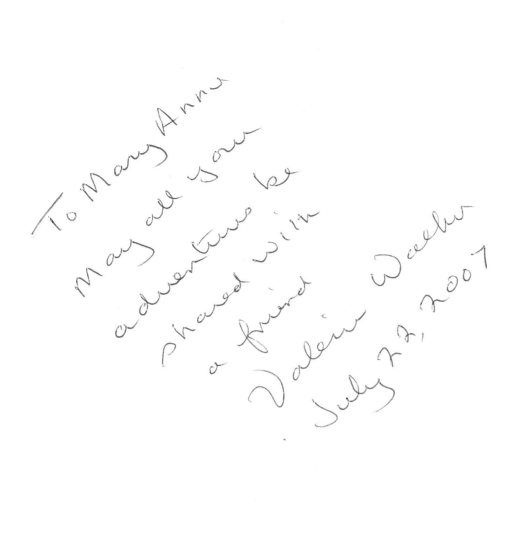

To Mary Anne
May all your
adventures be
shared with
a friend

Valerie Wheeler
July 22, 2007

The Adventures of Hedley the Hedgehog

by Valerie Walker

illustrated by Susan G. Waldie / edited by Terry Davies

Copyright © 1998 by Valerie Walker

Published by Valerie Walker
2634 6th Avenue N.W., Calgary, Alberta, Canada T2N 0X8

Copyright Registration No. 468092 / All rights reserved.

ISBN 0-9699587-0-6

Canadian Cataloguing in Publication Data

Walker, Valerie, 1937-
   The adventures of Hedley the hedgehog

   ISBN 0-9699587-0-6

   1. Waldie, Susan.   II. Title.
PS8595.A5598A73   1998   jC813'.54   C98-910227-0
PZ7.W15385Ad 1998

First Printing 1998

Design: Bulldog Communications / Printing: Friesen Printers
Printed and Bound in Canada

To Gerry for his
encouragement and support

———————————————

To my first-born grandchildren,
Marissa and David
who were the inspiration
for this book

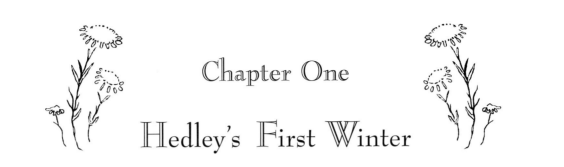

Chapter One

Hedley's First Winter

Under a hawthorn hedge, at the bottom of the vegetable garden, five young hedgehogs were preparing for winter.

"I'm making my nest in the middle of the hedge." said Spike.

"I'm making mine behind the garden shed." said Prickles.

"I'm making mine at the corner of the hedge." said Thorn. "And I'm making mine next to Thorn." said Thistle, who was the smallest of the five brothers.

"Where is your nest, Hedley?" asked Thorn.

"Yes, where?" asked Thistle.

Hedley was gazing at the sky. "Look, it's snowing, big, fluffy flakes." He stuck out his tongue. "-ook, -orn, -ey -elt on -y -ongue!" said Hedley, trying to speak while catching snowflakes.

"The first snow of winter." said Thorn. "We had better get on with building our nests."

"Finish our nests." said Thistle.

Hedley licked his lips. "I'm making my nest at the far end of the hawthorn hedge. There's a big pile of lovely dry leaves next to the compost heap, just perfect for a cosy nest. Bet I finish first!"

Hedley ran over to the pile of leaves and grass. He pulled them up against a thick branch and rolled on them. He rolled and rolled until they were all scrunched together, then just to be sure, he rolled some more.

"My nest is finished!" called Hedley. "Time to eat. I'm off to find some fat insects." He scurried off, leaves sticking to his spines. "Wibberly, wobberly, slickerly sloo, slugs and worms I'm looking for you!" sang Hedley as he ran down the path.

"I'm finished. Wait for me!" called Prickles.

"Me too!" said Thorn. "And me." added Thistle.

"Me too, well, almost." sighed Spike.

"Hurry up, slowpoke!" called Thorn. "Slowpoke." said Thistle.

At last, Spike was ready and the brothers set off for the vegetable garden.

Spike rooted among the winter cabbages. Thorn and Thistle sniffed around the last of the broccoli. Prickles snuffled at the parsnip leaves, and Hedley was ....exploring.

"I shall crawl under the house," he thought, "there are spiders and beetles under the porch." Smacking his lips, he wriggled beneath the steps. "It's awfully dark down here. I wonder if spiders can see in the dark?"

He sniffed along the ground then "Yuck!" he grunted as he ran into a spider web. "I think I'd rather be somewhere else!"

He hastily backed up and - bump! - sat down hard in a flower pot. Right tight in the pot. In fact, he was wedged so tight into that flower pot - he couldn't get out!

"Oh no," he moaned, "what do I do now?"

He wriggled. He squirmed. He dug his front feet into the dirt and pulled. But it was no use. He was stuck.

"Help!" he cried out weakly. "Help me, I'm stuck!"

He heard a scratching sound. It seemed to be coming nearer and nearer. He peered into the darkness and saw a dark shape looming towards him. Soon he was staring into a pair of yellow, unblinking eyes.

"Got yourself into a fine fix, haven't you?" said a voice. "Good thing I'm not a badger!"

"A badger!" Hedley shuddered thinking of his old enemy. "I'm very glad you're not a badger."

"No, but how do you know I'm not, hmmm?" said the voice.

"Because I would have smelled you." said Hedley. "Just who are you?"

The voice came nearer and Hedley could barely make out the shape coming towards him.

"I am Roger Rat. I live here. You are trespassing!"

"What does that mean?" asked Hedley.

"It means," hissed the rat, "that you shouldn't be here."

"Well, I don't really want to be here." said Hedley. "I was about to leave when I got stuck!"

"Yes." said the rat, circling Hedley slowly. "You certainly are."

"Do you have any suggestions as to how I can get out of here?" asked Hedley. "Please." he added as an afterthought.

"Well, I suppose I could make a few suggestions." said the rat.

"I would really appreciate it, er, Roger." said Hedley.

"Very well," sighed Roger, "can you crawl forward towards me?"

Hedley stuck his claws into the dirt and slowly edged forward.

"Like this?" he panted.

"Good. You'll have to crawl between the porch posts. The pot will get stuck, then out you'll pop."

Hedley puffed and panted and dragged himself, flower pot and all, up to the posts.

"There you are." said Roger. "Now dig in your front claws and pull as hard as you can. The pot should stay wedged between the posts. "

Hedley did as he was told. He took a deep breath, then pulled with all his might. Nothing. He tried again. He grunted and groaned and then, "pop!" out he came! He popped out so fast, he rolled right into Roger.

"Ouch, I say, watch those prickles will you?"

"I'm sorry, Roger," panted Hedley, "I hope I didn't hurt you?"

"No, just a scratch." said Roger, licking his side. "Well, you're out now, you had better be on your way. I don't want any of my pals seeing

me helping a hedgehog. Got my reputation to think of. Just keep going in this direction and you'll end up under the back steps. Now, be on your way, hurry up, scat!"

"Thank you for your kind help, Roger." said Hedley, as he very cautiously moved away.

Hedley crawled out into the fresh air and shook off the spiderwebs.

"Phew, that was a tight fix. Nice of Roger to help me. I'll not go under there again, I don't think his friends would be as helpful. That was thirsty work. I think it's time for a cool drink."

Hedley went around the back steps and was pleased to see the blue bowl, filled with delicious milk. He slurped thirstily. When the bowl was empty, he flipped it over with his paw.

"Just as I thought, lovely fat slugs."

He was so busy with his meal he didn't notice the humans watching him from the kitchen door.

"Look, Grandfather. How did that little hedgehog know there were slugs under the bowl?"

"I expect he can smell them, James." said Grandfather. "Hedgehogs need to eat a lot at this time of the year. They need to have a full tummy before they hibernate for the winter."

"How long do they hibernate, Grandfather?"

"Oh, probably till about April. As soon as the ground softens up and the bugs start moving again." replied Grandfather.

"I'm going to miss watching the hedgehogs come here to the back step and drink their milk in the evening." sighed James.

"Spring will be here soon enough, James. Then we must be ready to leave. As soon as the ground thaws, the big earth movers will arrive."

Grandfather picked up the newspaper and pointed to the front page.

November 4, 1920
'Local council to build new road............

"They will bulldoze the farmhouse, plough through the vegetable garden and dig up the hawthorn hedge. I'm glad we won't be around to see it, James." said Grandfather.

"Me too." said James, looking around the large Welsh kitchen. "I shall miss this old house. Grandfather, if the bulldozers dig up the hawthorn hedge, then that means the hedgehogs will lose their home. What will happen to them, where will they go?"

"They will have to find new homes, James. The young hoglets will be old enough to fend for themselves after hibernation."

"Grandfather, do you think we could take one of the hedgehogs with us to Somerset?" asked James.

Grandfather stroked his chin and looked at James. "Hedgehogs do like to roam." he murmered.

"Since they are going to lose their home anyway, I don't suppose it would hurt to take one with us. Which of the family of hedgehogs did you have in mind, James?"

"The one outside now, who just turned the bowl over. I see him wandering around on his own, exploring. Can we take him along with us please, Grandfather?"

"Why don't we wait till spring, James. If that young 'un is still as active and inquisitive after his long rest, and if you still feel the same, we can take him with us. I expect he would be quite content living on the farm."

"Oh thank you, Grandfather!" said James, "I will take really good care of the little hedgehog, I promise."

"Just remember, James, he is a wild creature and once we settle in, he must be free to make a home of his own." said Grandfather.

"I shall make him a traveling cot from an old shoebox." said James.

"There's plenty of time for that, lad. Now you had better get on and finish your homework."

James climbed the stairs to his bedroom, leaned on the window sill and looked down the path to the hawthorn hedge where the little hedgehog was slowly making his way home.

"Goodnight, little hedgehog," he whispered, "I'm glad you're coming with us to Somerset. I know we're going to have some fine adventures together. I can hardly wait to see my cousin Robert's face when he sees I have brought a friend with me."

James sighed to himself as he thought of the long winter ahead. "It seems such an awfully long time until spring."

Chapter Two

Hedley Meets James

Hedley opened one eye, slowly uncurled, stretched and opened the other eye. "Mmm," he thought, "what is that smell?"

His whiskers twitched and he snuffled around his leafy nest. "It's not in here, I had better look outside." He wriggled out from under the hawthorn hedge, took a deep breath and looked around.

"It must be spring." he thought. "The air smells fresh, there are shiny new leaves on the trees and..." his attention was caught by an earthworm disappearing into the ground, "it's time to eat! Wibberley, wobberly, slickery sloo, worms and slugs I'm looking for you!"

He ran back under the hawthorn hedge and called to his brothers. "Come on you lazy hedgehogs, it's spring! Hibernation is over. I'm going to the vegetable garden to look for some tasty slugs."

Thorn yawned. Thistle grunted. Prickles stretched. Spike grumbled. "It can't be spring already, I'm still tired."

"Me too," said Thorn, "but my tummy tells me it must be spring."

"Mine does too!" echoed Thistle.

"We had better hurry to the vegetable patch before Hedley eats all the fattest earthworms!" said Prickles.

The four sleepy hedgehogs left their nests and made their way to the vegetable garden. They saw Hedley turning over a broken flower pot.

"Why are you doing that?" asked Thorn. "Yes, why?" said Thistle.

"Because slugs like to hide under pots. They hide under stones too."

"Do you think there are some under here?" asked Thorn, as he and Thistle struggled to turn over a big stone. "How about under here?" said Prickles, flipping over another.

While Thorn, Thistle, Spike and Prickles were busy looking under stones, Hedley went exploring. A mother robin chirped from the bushes. "Stay away from my eggs, cheep, cheep."

Hedley moved on, his nose busy sniffing the ground. He heard a loud squeak and looked up to see a fieldmouse in his path.

"Where are you going?" squeaked the mouse.

"I'm exploring." said Hedley.

"There's a dish of milk by the kitchen door." said the mouse. "The young human put it out. He left some cheese too, but I ate that. Do you like cheese?"

"I don't think so," said Hedley, "but I do like milk. I shall go there right now. Thank you for telling me."

The mouse scurried off and Hedley made his way to the farmhouse. He stopped at the compost heap to chase an earthworm, sniffed at the woodpile for beetles and scratched under the rabbit hutch for grubs. He looked around and saw the familiar blue bowl beside the back step.

"The little mouse was right, the young human has put out milk." He slurped noisily from the bowl. He was just licking his chin, when the back door opened and the young human came out.

"Hello, little hedgehog." said the boy. "My name is James. I was hoping to see you. I watched you getting your nest ready for hibernation. May I pick you up? I won't hurt you, I promise."

The boy stroked Hedley's back very gently.

Hedley watched young James carefully. "He has eyes like the sky and a friendly voice. I like him." Hedley nudged the boy's hand. James picked up the little hedgehog and took him into the house.

Meanwhile Spike, Thorn, Thistle and Prickles were looking for Hedley.

"Do you think he's hiding?" asked Thorn. "You know Hedley always finds the best hiding places."

"The best." chimed in Thistle.

"Perhaps he is hiding in the compost heap." said Spike.

"Then let's go and look." said Prickles.

They looked in the compost and under the rabbit hutch. They looked around the woodpile, but Hedley wasn't in any of the usual places.

"Well, I'm tired of looking." said Thorn. "There's a bowl of milk by the door. All this searching has made me thirsty."

"Me too." said Thistle.

"I know where he is." piped up a little voice.

"Where?" said Thorn, looking up from the milk bowl. "Who said that?"

"Me." said the little mouse. "He is in the farmhouse. I saw the young human pick him up and take him inside."

"I just knew that Hedley's curiosity would get him into trouble!" said Thorn. "Big trouble!" said Thistle.

"What do you think will happen to him?" asked Prickles nervously.

"I don't know, but I think we had better go back to the hawthorn hedge." said Thorn. "To the hedge." said Thistle.

Inside the house, Hedley was having such an interesting time, he had almost forgotten about his brothers. James was showing Hedley around the large Welsh kitchen. There was a stone fireplace on one wall. A large iron pot hung from a hook over the fire.

A sudden movement caught Hedley's eye. He looked up to the mantle and saw the little mouse dart from behind a stack of books, then disappear behind a tobacco jar.

"We have to leave this house." James sighed. "They are going to build a road for these new motorcars. It will go right through the farm, the vegetable garden and your hawthorn hedge. That means you will lose your home also, little hedgehog."

"Lose my home." thought Hedley. "That means I can explore!"

James put Hedley on the kitchen table next to an old shoebox.

"We leave tomorrow for England." said James. "My uncle Giles and Aunt Jane have a farm in Somerset and we're going to live with them.

I shall go to school with my cousin Robert. After school, I will help Robert feed the pigs and weed the garden."

Hedley poked his head in the shoebox and looked around.

"It's a very large vegetable garden. Grandfather says we are going to need help keeping the bugs down. I was wondering, since we are both losing our homes, if you would like to come with us? I wouldn't feel so lonely if you were with me. We will be traveling by horse and cart. Grandfather doesn't like motorcars. He says they are noisy and dangerous. Please think about it, little hedgehog. It would be quite an adventure!"

"Adventure," thought Hedley, scratching his tummy, "traveling by horse and cart!" scratch, scratch. "Large vegetable garden." scratch, scratch, scratch. He ran in circles around the shoebox, then shook his bristles, ran up to James and licked his hand to let him know he thought it was a wonderful idea!

" Oh, I'm so glad you want to come little hedgehog! I am going to call you Hedley. It was my Father's name. What do you think of that, Hedley?"

"Well, fancy his father having the same name as me," thought Hedley, "of course I think it is a perfect name."

James picked up Hedley and stroked him again. "I am so glad you are coming with us. I'll take you back to the hawthorn hedge so you can see your family."

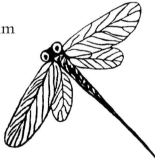

James carried Hedley to the vegetable garden, where his brothers were gathered. He set him down, then sat quietly while they talked.

"Hedley, you gave us quite a scare. Where have you been?" asked Thorn.

"With him?" asked Thistle bravely, as he stared up at James.

"Yes little Thistle, I have been with James. He has asked me to go to England with him and his Grandfather. We leave tomorrow. Thorn, it will be such an adventure!"

"You mean, you are going to leave us?" asked Spike.

"There is a road going through here. Our hedge will be torn down. We shall all have to find new homes." said Hedley.

"Find a new home?" said Thorn. "But I like it here!"

"Me too!" said Thistle. "So do I!" added Spike.

"There are other farms, Thorn. I'm sure you will all find homes closeby. I know you would like to stay here, but I want to travel. Do you remember the stories about our great grandfather? He went up to the north country and had lots of exciting adventures!"

"Yes," said Thorn, "and if you remember, he came to a sticky end. Fell off the roof into a vat of tar!"

"Hot tar!" said Thistle.

"I heard he drowned trying to swim the Irish Sea!" said Spike.

"The way I heard it, he was run over by a large steam roller till he was flat as a pancake!" said Prickles.

"Those were just stories to scare us into staying close to home." said Hedley.

"Well, staying close to home sounds just fine to me!" said Thorn. "I shall probably move over to the farm next door. They have a bushy hedge, just like this one."

"I'll go with Thorn." said Thistle.

"And I'll go to the farm on the west side. They have a hog-sized vegetable garden." said Spike. "Where will you go, Prickles?"

"Oh, I'll probably go to the house by the stream." said Spike. "I find the sound of running water very restful."

"You see?" said Hedley. "You will all be just fine on your own."

"I suppose so," sighed Thorn, "but we'll miss you Hedley."

"Miss you." said Thistle.

"I shall miss you too." said Hedley.

"Are you sure it's safe to go with humans?" asked Prickles.

"I'm quite sure," said Hedley, "James and Grandfather are very kind."

"What kind of place are you going to?" asked Spike.

"It's a farm, like this, only much bigger. James said I will be a big help in the vegetable garden."

"I'm sure you will." said Thorn. "You are the best at finding slugs and worms, Hedley. I shall remember what you said about looking under flower pots and rocks."

"We shall." said Thistle.

"Take care of yourself." said Prickles, sniffing.

"Have a fine adventure." said Spike, blinking very hard.

"Thank you, I shall. And I know you will find comfortable homes." said Hedley. "Come and visit me anytime."

Then he turned away and, sniffing loudly, walked with James back to the farmhouse.

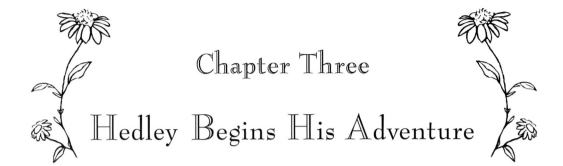

Chapter Three

Hedley Begins His Adventure

The next morning, Hedley was bursting with excitement. He crawled from the shoebox and wriggled his nose. He was in the middle of a long stretch when he heard a little voice.

"Good morning." squeaked the mouse. "So you are off on an adventure?"

"Yes." replied Hedley, looking around the kitchen. The little mouse was sitting above the large stone fireplace.

"I heard the young human call you Hedley, my name is Marvin."

"Good morning to you, Marvin." said Hedley. "Have you ever been on a great adventure?"

"No," replied the mouse, "but I think I might go on one today!" and he scurried away as James and his Grandfather came into the room.

"So you are to be our new companion, Hedley." said Grandfather. "Pleased to have you along. You'll be a big help in the vegetable garden."

Hedley looked up into a brown, smiling face. "Rather like a wrinkled winter apple." thought Hedley. "He has the same twinkly blue eyes as James, but his hair is white and fluffy - like a dandelion before the wind blows it away."

"Now, James," said Grandfather, "we have a busy morning ahead of us. Let's have breakfast and load the cart."

James set out cat food and water for Hedley. "I hope you like this, Hedley, Grandfather says it's time you were weaned from milk."

Hedley munched on his breakfast while James helped his Grandfather. "Hmm, smells good," he thought, "tasty too!" He was about to lick the last of the food from the dish, when he saw Marvin peering at him from behind the chair. "You look hungry, Marvin, I'll leave the rest for you."

Marvin crept towards the dish. "Why thank you, Hedley. Cat food is one of my favourite treats." He had just finished when Grandfather and James came into the kitchen with more boxes. Marvin scurried off to the safety of the chair and watched.

The neighbour, Mrs. Jones came in to help. Her long skirt brushed the chair, and out came Marvin.

"Eek!" she shrieked. "A mouse!"

"Eek!" Marvin squealed. " A human!"

Marvin scurried out the door and hid under the step. He watched Grandfather and James loading boxes onto the cart. "James isn't afraid of mice. Grandfather isn't afraid of mice. Hedley isn't afraid of mice. And I'm not afraid of them! Maybe it's time I had an adventure!"

Marvin waited until James and Grandfather had gone back into the house. Then, quick as a flash, he ran to the cart, scrambled up the wheel, over the side and hid among the packages.

James came back into the kitchen. "What do you think of the shoebox, Hedley? Is it comfortable? I lined it with moss and cut a hole for you. I thought you could travel in it."

"It's very cosy," thought Hedley, "as long as I don't have to stay in it for too long!"

"Don't worry, little Hedley. We'll make lots of stops on the way so you can get out and stretch." said James.

Hedley crawled in and out of the shoebox several times, sat on the table, shook his bristles and scratched his ear. "As long as I can get out and explore when we stop," thought Hedley, "it will do very well."

At last they were ready to leave. James climbed onto the cart and tucked Hedley into the shoebox. "Now our adventure begins, Hedley." said James as he placed the shoebox beside him on the seat.

Grandfather took up the reins and urged Ned the horse forward. They waved goodbye to Mrs. Jones, and were off.

Hedley was very excited. From his shoebox, he could see over the fields and hedges. "The world looks so different!" he thought. "I can see the top of the haystacks. I can see the top of the barn! At last, I'm on a real adventure!"

Soon, they passed through a little Welsh village. The road was very narrow. Hedley heard a familiar sound, "Baa, baa, baa." Grandfather stopped the cart to let the herd of sheep make their way by.

"They don't look so big from here!" thought Hedley. As he watched, a sheep dog nipped at their heels to keep them in line. "I'm glad I'm up here, dogs make me very nervous."

"Won't be long before shearing starts." said Grandfather. "Good Welsh wool, that's what your sweater is made from, James."

Once the sheep had passed, Grandfather shook the reins and Ned pulled the cart back onto the narrow road.

Hedley was daydreaming and wondering what his brothers were doing, when he noticed the scenery changing. There were lots of houses on each side of the road and strange machines were racing up and down the street. "Honk, Honk!"

"Those must be the motorcars Grandfather was talking about." thought Hedley. "Noisy things!"

"We're coming into town now, James, too much traffic for my liking." said Grandfather. Hedley agreed.

"I wonder if any hedgehogs live here?" He was thinking about what life would be like in such a busy place when Grandfather said, "We are about to cross the river Severn, then we'll be in England."

Hedley wanted to see the river. It was moving very fast, much faster than the little stream he was used to on the farm.

"Look at those big barges! Grandfather!" said James. "What sort of things could they be carrying?"

"Coal, most likely." said Grandfather.

Hedley had never seen barges before, but he knew what coal was. He had often hidden in the coal bin when he and his brothers were playing hide and seek.

The tug that was hauling the barges gave a loud "Toot, toot" on its horn. Hedley rolled into a tight ball.

"Poor Hedley," said James, "the noise must have frightened him. He looks like a prickly chestnut!"

"That's how hedgehogs defend themselves, James. They curl up and stick out their bristles."

Hedley slowly straightened himself out, peered around, and then looked up into James' smiling face.

"Don't worry, Hedley, we're nearly off the bridge. How long till we get to Uncle Giles' farm, Grandfather?"

"Depends, lad. Maybe we will be there the day after tomorrow."

"That's a long time to be in a shoebox." said James.

"Just what I was thinking." muttered Hedley to himself.

Grandfather was happy to get out of the town and onto a quiet country road. "Why don't you have a little rest, James. We'll stop at the next Inn for supper, then you and Hedley can run around and explore."

"Good idea," said James, "I am feeling a little sleepy." James placed the shoebox safely between a large tea chest and suitcase, and settled down for a sleep.

"I think I'll curl up in the corner." thought Hedley. "Maybe I'll have a little nap before we go exploring." He rolled up into the moss and tucked his nose between his paws.

Ned was happy to be out of the town. He shook his head and snorted. Grandfather smiled. "You want to move a little faster, Ned?"

He shook the reins and encouraged Ned to change into a gentle trot. "That's better, we both prefer the countryside don't we old boy?"

Hedley started to roll back and forth in the shoebox. He thought it quite pleasant at first, but it soon became rougher and rougher. He rolled around faster and faster, until the lid flew off the shoebox. Hedley rolled out, bounced over the parcels and packages, bump, bump, bump, right off the end of the cart!

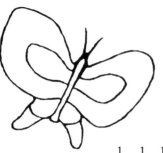

Dazed and trembling, Hedley uncurled and opened his eyes. There, disappearing over the hill, was the horse and cart! He squinted his eyes against the sun.

"It looks as if something else fell off." he thought. He blinked a few times and looked again. "Well, I do believe it is that friendly little mouse. He must have hidden among the parcels."

The mouse scampered up to Hedley. "Well, I didn't expect you to be leaving so soon. What do we do now, Hedley?"

"Marvin, am I glad to see you. I fell off the cart when Ned started to trot. I suppose we shall have to try and follow them." He gave himself a good shake and made his way to the side of the road, followed by Marvin.

"Well, I said I wanted an adventure, so let's go!" They hadn't gone far when Hedley heard a heavy panting behind him. He immediately rolled into a ball and stuck out his prickles.

A scruffy, black dog with wiry hair and a floppy tail came up and sniffed at Hedley.

"Sniff, sniff, sniff - yipe!" The little hedgehog was a ball of prickles! The dog then batted Hedley with its paw and yelped again. Deciding that the hedgehog probably didn't taste very good anyway, the dog wisely left, his tail between his legs.

"That was a neat trick!" said Marvin, appearing from under a patch of clover. "How did you do that? You really scared away that old dog. Do you think you could show me how to curl up?"

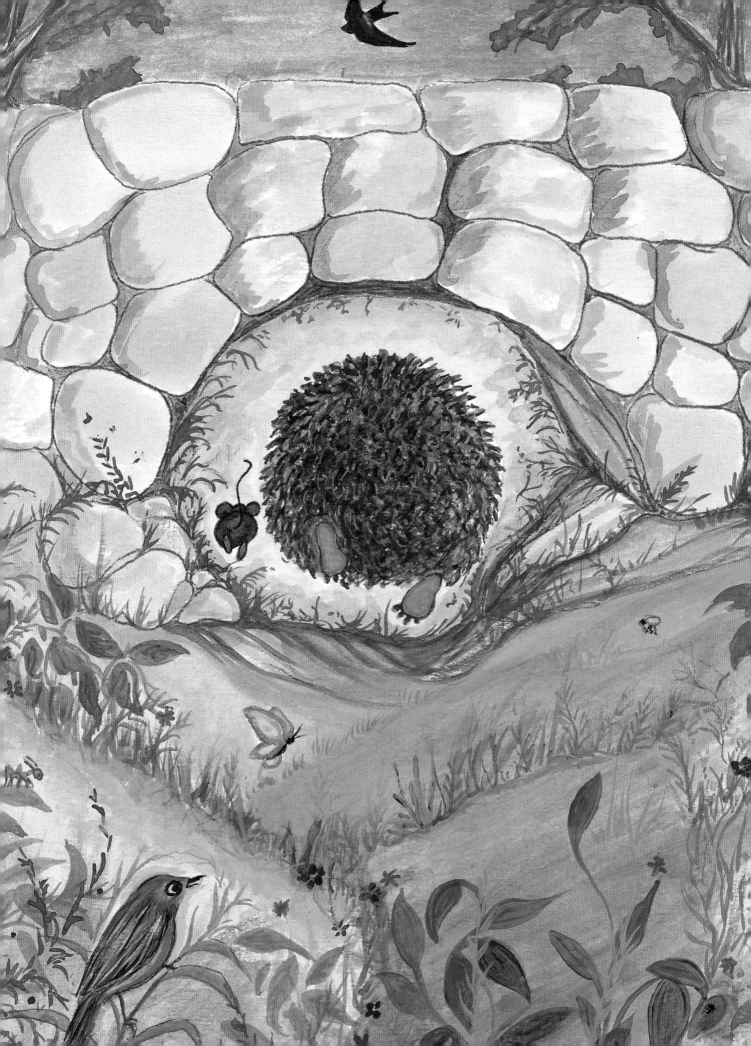

"It's easy," said Hedley, "for hedgehogs anyway. I don't know about a mouse though. Try tucking your head onto your belly and………….." Hedley rolled into a ball. Marvin tucked his head down. "Ow, ouch, ow! No, you're right," said Marvin after several attempts to curl up, "it doesn't work that way for mice."

With all the excitement, Hedley had almost forgotten that the cart was getting further and further away. "Come on, Marvin, we must hurry if we want to catch up." said Hedley. "I think it would be safer to travel in the ditch. I don't want to meet any of those dangerous new motorcars."

"Me neither." said Marvin, as the friends set off to follow the cart.

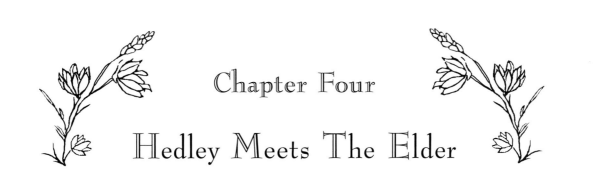

Chapter Four

Hedley Meets The Elder

Hedley felt more cheerful with Marvin by his side. "I'm glad you decided to join me, Marvin, adventures are so much better when they are shared. Would you like to hear a song?"

"I'd love to." answered the little mouse.

Hedley cleared his throat and started to sing.

"If trouble comes to call,
just roll into a ball.

If you are in a pickle,
stick out your spiny prickles.

If you..............................."

"You there. What's that you're singing?"

Hedley looked around. The voice seemed to be coming from a hedge.

"Who are you, I say? Just what do you think you are doing running around in the middle of the day disturbing my sleep?"

Hedley turned to ask Marvin if he could see who was speaking, but the little mouse was nowhere to be seen.

"I've never seen you in these parts before. You're not from around here. What's your name ...... Well, speak up. Cat got your tongue?"

Hedley looked around again, then noticed the frowning face of an old hedgehog looking at him through the bushes.

"Where are your manners, young 'un? Don't you know how to treat your elders?" The old hedgehog came out from the bushes and stood glaring at Hedley.

"Sorry, sir, I didn't know you were there. My name is Hedley."

"Hedley!" said the Elder, "What sort of name is that?"

"A very good name," said Hedley, bristling, "a good Welsh name."

"Ah, Welsh are you? No wonder I haven't seen you around here. Don't you know you are in England now?"

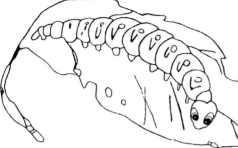

"Yes I know, sir. I am on my way to Somerset with ...."

"Somerset!" roared the Elder, "Now why do you want to go there? What's wrong with staying right here in Gloucester?"

"Well, sir, I was traveling with James and Grandfather, when the horse, Ned started to trot and I rolled out of my box and fell off the cart and............"

"Fell off the cart! Traveling with humans! What on earth were you doing traveling with humans, anyway?"

"James, the little boy, invited me to go on an adventure with him. He made a cozy home for me in an old shoebox and................."

"IN A SHOEBOX!" roared the Elder. "What is the world coming to when young hoglets make their homes in shoeboxes?"

"It's only while we are traveling." explained Hedley. "When we get to the new farm, I shall live in the vegetable garden."

The Elder shook his head and muttered to himself about foolish young hedgehogs traveling with humans around the countryside.

Hedley thought perhaps he should just slip away.

"And just where do you think you are going?" the old hedgehog said.

"I thought perhaps I had better be on my way. It's quite far and I need to catch up to them before nightfall............."

"You mean you still want to find these humans?" asked the Elder.

"Of course, sir," said Hedley, "they invited me to go with them and I agreed. It would be bad manners to break my promise."

"Bah, they have probably forgotten about you. You would do better to stay here. We need bright young hoglets like you."

"That is very kind of you, sir," said Hedley, "but I really must be on my way now. They will be worried about me."

"Hrmph!" said the Elder. "If that's the way you feel, then I suppose you had better go. I am glad to hear you keep your word. A promise is a promise. Maybe I can help you find your friends."

The Elder sat thinking, muttering to himself. He scratched behind his ear with his back paw. Then he scratched under his chin with his front paw. Finally he gave a long shake, wriggled his nose and said. "Wait here, I have an idea." The old hedgehog disappeared back into the bushes.

"He's not such a bad fellow after all." squeaked Marvin, creeping out from behind a rock. "His bark is worse than his bite."

"There you are, Marvin. I thought you had deserted me."

"Just being cautious." twitched the little mouse. "You know, I don't have any prickles. How do you think he can help us?"

"I don't know." said Hedley. "I suppose we shall just have to wait and see." The two friends sat side by side. "I wonder where this adventure is going to lead us next?" thought Marvin to himself.

Hedley was drinking from a puddle when the old hedgehog reappeared, followed by a handsome grey rabbit.

"This is Conrad." said the Elder. "He's a very smart fellow and he has an excellent idea."

"How do you do, Hedley. Pleased to meet you"... twitch - twitch...,"meet you." said Conrad, repeating himself. "Welcome to Gloucester."

"How do you do, Conrad. It's a pleasure to meet you." said Hedley as he watched the nervous twitching of the rabbit's whiskers.

"Never mind all this small talk," interrupted the Elder, "let's hear what Conrad has to say. Now, you listen carefully to this young 'un."

"We rabbits," said Conrad, "have a way of communicating with each other. I'll send a message to my cousin to watch the road for your friends. He could get their attention," ... twitch - twitch..., "attention."

"How very clever of you," said Hedley, fascinated with the rabbit's busy nose, "however do you do it? Is it hard to do?"

"Twitch my whiskers?" asked Conrad, "It's easy, you just........."

"No, no." said Hedley, feeling rather embarrassed. "I meant, how do you communicate with your friends?"

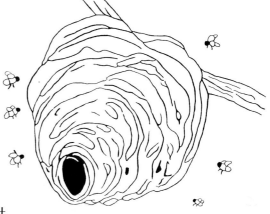

"Like this" ...twitch – twitch said Conrad, "you must be very quiet and give me lots of room. I need lots of room."

Hedley, Marvin and the Elder backed up and watched as Conrad closed his eyes. Hedley thought the rabbit had gone to sleep, when suddenly, Conrad's large rear foot started thumping loudly on the ground.

"Thump, thump - thump, thump!" Startled, Hedley curled up. Soon, he heard a faint thumping coming from far away. He uncurled and crept a little closer so he could hear better.

Conrad listened intently, then sent off another round of thumps. They all sat quietly staring at Conrad. Then, there was an answer. "There." he said opening his eyes. "They have passed on the message. They will get back to me soon,"... twitch - twitch..., " very soon."

"How are they going to stop James and Grandfather?" asked Hedley.

"My cousin is going to run out in front of the cart to get the horse's attention. The Grandfather will then get off the cart to see why the horse has stopped." replied Conrad.

"What will happen then?" asked the Elder.

"Oh, James will jump down to make sure the rabbit is alright. He'll notice that I am missing. Then they'll turn around and come looking for me." interrupted Hedley.

"Precisely!" said Conrad.

"I just hope the humans are smart enough to follow your rabbit back here." said the Elder. "They don't have our instincts you know."

Hedley was about to assure the Elder that they were very smart, when he heard thumping in the distance. Conrad listened quietly, then bounced up and down. "He has spotted them. He did it. The cart is turning around!"... twitch - twitch...,"Around!"

Hedley was delighted. "Oh, thank you, Conrad. You were wonderful. You too, Elder, sir. You have both been very kind. Would you like to meet my young friend James and his Grandfather?"

"Gracious, no!" said the Elder. "I'm too old to start getting mixed up with humans. I shall watch from the hedge over there to make sure they pick you up safely."

"What about you, Conrad," asked Hedley, "would you like to meet them? I'm sure they would like to meet you."

"Oh dear, no," replied Conrad, "I am very nervous around humans. I'll just watch with the Elder." He hopped off into the bushes, leaving the Elder to say goodbye to Hedley.

"I can see the old cart coming." said the Elder. "Good luck, Hedley! One day you'll be able to tell your own young 'uns about your adventure." and he shuffled after Conrad.

"Thank you both for your help. I'll never forget you!" called Hedley. "You are very kind." Then he turned and ran towards the cart with the little mouse following closely behind him.

"There he is, Grandfather!" cried James, "I knew we would find him. Oh, Hedley, I'm so glad to see you! We thought you were lost. If that little rabbit hadn't run out and scared Ned, we wouldn't have known you were missing." James picked up Hedley and took him back to show Grandfather.

"Well, he seems to be all in one piece." said Grandfather. "I wonder if that little rabbit had something to do with this. I wouldn't be surprised if Hedley had some help from the forest creatures. Look, there are two pairs of eyes watching from the hedge."

"I think you're right, Grandfather." James turned towards the hedge and waved. "Thank you, whoever you are!"

While James was busy with Hedley, Marvin ran up the wheel of the cart and hid among the packages. "Well, so far this has been very exciting." he thought. "What could possibly happen next?"

James tucked Hedley back into the shoebox. He set the shoebox firmly between Grandfather and himself. "There. Now we can be sure he won't fall out." he said.

"I think we've had enough excitement for one day, James." sighed Grandfather, urging Ned forward. "We'll stop at the next Inn, it's just a little further down the road. We could both use a hot meal and a good night's sleep. We still have a long journey ahead of us."

"Good idea." thought Hedley. "Adventuring is tiring. I'm feeling quite sleepy." and he curled up in his shoebox for a nap.

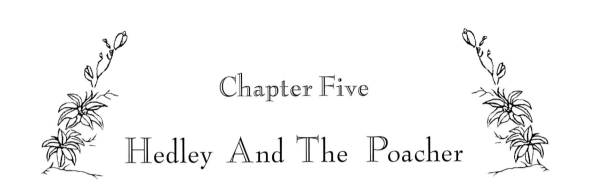

Chapter Five

Hedley And The Poacher

Hedley was enjoying the view from the circular window of his shoebox. It was a sunny morning and the birds were singing.

"The air smells sweet, Grandfather." said James.

"Ah, now," said Grandfather, "that would be the May trees in bloom. Sweet smelling, they are. Look, there are bluebells in the woods yonder."

James held up the box so that Hedley could see. The sudden movement startled Hedley and he rolled into a ball. "I'm sorry I frightened you, Hedley, now you're going to miss the flowers." said James.

"Will we see more bluebells, Grandfather?"

"I certainly hope so, lad." the old man replied. "Listen now, do you hear the cuckoo? That's a sure sign of spring."

James sat quietly and listened. "Yes, I do hear him. That's just what he is singing-cuckoo, cuckoo!"

Talking about birds made Hedley think of worms. "Worms! Yummy. Beetles! Yummy. Slugs! Yummy, yummy!"

"We'll stop at the top of the next hill to give old Ned a rest." said Grandfather. "I'm feeling a little hungry, how about you, James?"

"Mm - yes, I was just thinking of the nice thick slices of bread and cheese the Innkeeper packed for our lunch. Could we can find a spot for a picnic and let Hedley out for a snack?"

"Wonderful idea." thought Hedley.

Ned plodded slowly up the long hill. When they reached the top, Grandfather gave Ned a bag of oats. James set out a blanket and a basket of food under a shady oak tree. He gently lifted Hedley from his box and placed him under a nearby hedge.

"There you are Hedley, now you can have a good stretch but don't wander too far away. We won't be here very long." said James.

Hedley wriggled his nose and gave his bristles a shake to indicate he understood, then set out to search for his favourite food. Marvin, who was waiting beside the picnic basket, called out "Wait for me!"

He followed Hedley who was moving from bush to bush, happily searching out bugs, "Wibberly, wobberly, slickery sloo, worms and slugs I'm looking for you!"

He had just finished singing his little rhyme when he heard a whimpering nearby.

Hedley moved towards the sound and saw to his horror a young rabbit with its foot caught in a snare. He was trembling with fear and stared nervously at Hedley with big brown eyes.

"Don't be afraid, little rabbit. We're not going to hurt you, are we, Marvin?" Hedley looked around but Marvin was nowhere to be seen.

"My name is Hedley. What is yours?"

"Ch..Chester, can you help me please?"

"The rope looks pretty tough, but I'll give it a try."

Hedley was so busy chewing away at the snare, that he didn't notice the shadow of the poacher fall over him.

A sack dropped over his head.

"Gotcha !" said a gruff voice.

Hedley was struggling to get out. The sack was opened and Chester came tumbling in on top of him. They barely had time to catch their breath, when they were lifted in the air and bumped together again as the poacher swung the bag over his shoulder.

Marvin, who had been hiding under a fallen log, watched in dismay as Hedley and the little rabbit were carried away. "I'd better follow them - from a safe distance, of course. I may be able to help - somehow."

Looking nervously about, Marvin left the safety of the log and, darting from tree to tree, followed the poacher.

"Oh dear, I'm so sorry you got caught too." said Chester.

"Caught, what do you mean?" asked Hedley.

"The poacher, he's been chasing me all morning. I though I was safe until I got my foot caught in that snare."

"Why does he want to catch us?" asked Hedley, "Just what do you think he is going to do with us?"

"Why, he wants to eat us, of course!" replied Chester.

"Eat us!" exclaimed Hedley. "Not if I can help it. How is your foot, Chester? Can you hop around on it?"

"Well, nothing seems to be broken." said Chester. "Just a little sore."

"Good." said Hedley. "Now we must find a way to get out. How are you at nibbling through sacking, Chester? Perhaps if you start chewing a hole at one corner and I start at the other corner, we could make holes big enough for both of us to escape."

While Hedley and Chester were busy nibbling away at the sack, James and Grandfather were getting ready to leave.

"Hedley!" called James. "We're ready to go now, where are you?"

He walked over to the hedge where he had last seen Hedley and called again. No sign of him anywhere. Grandfather joined in the search. They looked high and low, but Hedley was nowhere to be seen.

"Hello, what's this?" Grandfather exclaimed. James ran over to see what his grandfather was looking at.

"What is it Grandfather?"

"It's a snare, James. Recently used, I'd say."

"Oh, Grandfather, I'm worried about Hedley. Do you think a poacher has got him?"

"It's possible, James. There are poachers around these parts. We'll just have to see if we can find any tracks. There seems to be a path leading into the woods. Maybe we should follow it and see what we find."

By this time, Hedley and Chester had chewed fair sized holes in each corner of the sack.

"The hole's not quite big enough for you to squeeze through, Chester," whispered Hedley, "keep on chewing, we'll soon be out of here."

The poacher reached his little shack in a clearing and lay the sack on the ground. He started to prepare a fire. "My, those two critters are going to make a fine meal." he chuckled.

"That's what he thinks." muttered Hedley. "He is going to be in for a big surprise!"

Meanwhile, James and Grandfather had caught sight of a thin trickle of smoke curling up between the trees. "If I'm not mistaken," said Grandfather, "this is where the trail ends."

"Oh, Grandfather, there's the poacher. He's gathering a pile of wood. You don't think we are too late, do you?" James asked.

"No lad, I'm pretty sure he has just started the fire." he said as they crept closer and hid in the bushes.

Hedley cautiously poked his head through the hole in the sack and looked around. "That's strange, I thought I saw my little friend Marvin hiding in the woodpile." He shook his head and looked again. "It is Marvin! He must have followed us. Brave little fellow!"

The little mouse looked both ways, then made a mad dash for the sack. "Oh, Hedley, I'm so glad you are safe. You too, Chester. I was so scared when the poacher caught you, I thought I would never see you again. I decided to follow to see if I could help. Do you need help, Hedley? I have very sharp teeth you know, see?" Marvin grinned widely, showing his tiny white teeth.

"I am so happy to see you, Marvin." said Hedley. "It took a great deal of courage for you to come after us. Perhaps you could help Chester while I check on the poacher."

While Marvin and Chester gnawed at the sack, Hedley poked his head out and looked around for the poacher.

"We are facing the woods. The poacher is busy with his fire and has his back to us. This may be our only chance to escape, so listen carefully.

When you get out of the sack, make straight for the trees. Don't stop for anything until you are safe. Is the hole big enough?"

Chester nodded. "Thanks to Marvin."

" I'll count to three, then we'll all make a dash for it. Are you ready?"

"Ready." said Chester, his whiskers twitching nervously.

"Ready." said Marvin, making himself as small as possible.

"Right." said Hedley. "One, Two, Three!"

Hedley squeezed through the hole, blinked, and ran as fast as he could to the safety of the trees. Chester followed, hopping around in confusion.

"Over here! This way!" cried Hedley.

Chester gave a frightened glance towards the poacher, then bounded after Hedley, closely followed by Marvin.

"There he is, James!" said Grandfather, stepping quietly out of the bush.

Hedley ran to Grandfather and safety. When poor Chester saw Grandfather walking towards him he squealed in fright.

"Eeps, another human!" and dashed down the nearest hole. Marvin almost followed him, then remembered he wasn't afraid of Grandfather.

"At least the little rabbit got away." sighed James. He picked up Hedley and, together with Grandfather, crept back to the horse and cart. Marvin followed at a safe distance. Just as Grandfather took up Ned's reins, they heard a loud bellow from the poacher.

"Yaaaa!"

"Ha! There'll be no lunch for that old chappie today!" Grandfather laughed as he helped James and Hedley onto the cart.

"I do hope the little rabbit is alright. He looked awfully frightened." said James.

"I hope so too." thought Hedley.

Grandfather led Ned back onto the road. "I'm sure he'll be fine. In fact, isn't that him over there in the ditch?"

James lifted Hedley up so he could see.

"Yes, that's him, that's Conrad!" thought Hedley, "Now he's safe and sound." Hedley blinked and wriggled his nose.

Chester blinked back, then turned and popped into another hole.

"I would say Hedley and his friend had quite a close shave, James," said Grandfather, "but all's well that ends well. Now we had better be going. We still have a long way to go before we reach the farm." He shook the reins and urged Ned into a gentle trot.

Marvin was struggling through the long grass and just managed to scramble aboard the cart as Grandfather pulled away.

A little head poked out of the bushes.

"Goodbye, Hedley. Good luck on your travels."

Chester watched as the cart rumbled off into the distance, then turned and headed for the safety of his own burrow.

Chapter Six

Hedley Makes A New Friend

Hedley awoke with a start. He had been dreaming of his brothers and was feeling a little sad. He was so far from home and so many things had happened. Then, he caught a whiff of something in the air.

He poked his nose through the hole in the shoebox to see what was happening. "The air smells different," he thought, "but it's very familiar. Of course, it smells like the farm back in Wales!"

"Nearly there, James!" said Grandfather. "When we reach the top of this hill we'll be able to see our new home."

James held Hedley closer to him. "Did you hear that, Hedley, we're almost there! We're almost at our new home!"

Hedley was as excited as James. "Oh, it will be grand to be able to run around again! I'm feeling quite stiff from all this traveling."

As they pulled into the farmyard, chickens clucked and fluttered away. Piglets squealed and ducks quacked.

"What a busy place this is!" thought Hedley. Grandfather got down from the cart and led Ned to the water trough.

"Are you ready to meet your Aunt Jane and Uncle Giles, lad?" he asked.

James nodded, holding Hedley tightly against his chest.

"Maybe it would be a good idea to leave Hedley on the cart for now. We can come back for him later." said Grandfather.

James set Hedley carefully onto the back of the cart. "Stay there Hedley. We won't be very long." James slid his hand into his Grandfather's as they walked towards the house.

The door flew open and Aunt Jane bustled down the steps, wiping flour-covered hands on her apron.

"Good gracious, you're here sooner than I expected. Oh, but how you have grown, James!" She smothered him in a big hug, leaving flour on his nose and cheeks.

Grandfather chuckled and patted Aunt Jane lovingly on the shoulder. "How about a hug and kiss for your dear old Dad, then?"

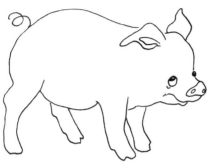

Aunt Jane released James from her embrace and turned to welcome him.

"My, Dad, it is so good to see you. We are really glad you decided to come and live with us. Young Robert is anxious to see James again. He's just down at the hen house feeding the chickens. Why don't you go and find him, James?"

James darted off to go and look for his cousin.

Hedley was quite excited and anxious to explore his new surroundings.

"I wonder how long they will be? They could be gone for a long time. Maybe I could just get down from here and have a look around." He stood and looked over the edge of the cart.

"Hmm, it's quite a long way down. Maybe I could curl up into a ball and just roll off without hurting myself."

He was fidgeting at the edge of the cart when he noticed a strange creature with horns trotting towards him.

"Beh, beh, are you good to eat?" bleated the creature.

"Eat? Certainly not. I'm full of prickles, see!" Hedley curled up and expanded his spines. The billy goat backed away in surprise.

"You're a strange looking animal! How did you do that?" he asked.

"I am a hedgehog." said Hedley, "We curl up and stick out our prickles when we're in danger, and I seem to be in danger of being eaten by you!"

"Oh, I don't really want to eat you. That's just my little joke. I have a reputation to live up to, you know."

"What's that?" asked Hedley.

"That I'll eat anything!" bleated the goat. "Newspapers, laundry off the line, empty cartons, that sort of thing. My name is Billy. What's yours?"

"Hedley. Pleased to meet you, Billy, I think."

"Why are you standing at the edge of a cart full of packages?" asked Billy. "Are you waiting there for someone?"

"I am waiting for James. He and Grandfather are visiting with their family, and I feel the need to stretch my legs." said Hedley.

"I should think so." said Billy. "Maybe I can help. I could lift you down in my mouth. Of course, you would have to keep your prickles in. What do you say? Is that alright with you?"

Hedley wasn't so sure. He had only just met Billy and he didn't know much about goats, except they would eat anything. "Alright, Billy. I trust you, but please be gentle. Your teeth look awfully strong."

"Oh, they are strong teeth." said Billy, "Very, very strong. I can crush a tin can in my mouth with no trouble at all."

"On second thought," said Hedley, "maybe I'll just stay here."

"Don't be silly. I promise I won't hurt you."

Hedley thought about it for a moment. He nodded briefly, then curled up and flattened his spines. He felt a gentle pressure on his body and before he knew it, he was on the ground.

"You can uncurl those prickles now!" laughed Billy, "You are safe and sound. Safe and sound with Billy around!"

Hedley shook himself. "Thank you, Billy. It feels good to get off that cart."

"Would you like me to show you the farm?" asked Billy. "It's a great place."

"Yes, please." said Hedley.

"Watch out for those ducklings." warned Billy as they stepped aside to let the babies catch up with their mother.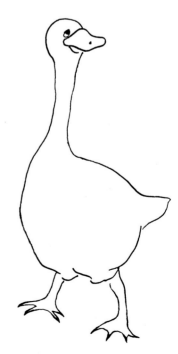

"Here come the piglets."

"Oink, oink." The pudgy piglets chased back and forth after the ducklings.

"It's like this every spring. You have to really watch where you're stepping."

"Yes, I see," said Hedley as he moved aside for a little yellow chick, "it certainly is a busy place around here. Would you mind showing me where the vegetable garden is please, Billy?"

"I'd be happy to," Billy replied, "it's just over here."

"Wait for me!" a little voice squeaked. Hedley and Billy turned around just as Marvin ran up to join them.

"Billy, this is Marvin. He used to live at grandfather's farmhouse in Wales."

"I thought I saw a mouse on the cart. I hope I didn't scare you." said Billy.

"Scared? Me, scared? Of course not! Hedley and I have been on a grand adventure, and we're not afraid of anything now, are we, Hedley?"

"That's right, Marvin." replied Hedley.

"As long as you don't pick me up in your mouth, Billy!" said Marvin.

"I promise." said Billy and the three friends walked along together until they came to the vegetable garden. Hedley was pleasantly surprised.

"It's twice as big as the garden we had in Wales!" he said in awe. "There must be plenty of slugs, worms and caterpillars hiding among the cauliflower leaves."

"Can't say the idea of eating wiggly worms and slimy slugs appeals to me." said Billy. "Must taste worse than wellington boots! Very rubbery they are – and hard to digest. The humans were quite upset when I ate their wellies. However, they seem very pleased with me when I eat the grass."

"Speaking for myself," squeaked Marvin, "I find lots of tasty treats that humans throw away. Of course, I don't mean in the house." he added hastily. "I think the compost heap is a great place to find an interesting meal. See you later!"

And with that, the little mouse scampered off to the pile of discarded kitchen scraps in the corner of the garden.

Hedley watched his little friend. Suddenly, he noticed that there was a hedge next to the compost heap. His mouth gaped open.

"What are you looking at?" asked Billy.

"Over there," sighed Hedley, "a beautiful, bushy hawthorn hedge."

"What's so special about a hawthorn hedge?" asked Billy.

"I lived under a hawthorn hedge in Wales." said Hedley. "I was born there and so were my brothers." Thinking of his brothers made Hedley feel sad and a little tear appeared at the corner of his eye.

He sniffed. The garden smelled of onions. The delicious odor made him smile through his tears. "It looks like the perfect place for me."

Hedley wove his way through the lettuce and spinach. He sniffed around the carrots and brussel sprouts. He dodged between the rows of beans until he stood before the hawthorn hedge.

"Just look, Billy. The hedge is in full bloom! The flowers are so pretty and they smell good, too! ....Mmmmmm."

"Taste delicious." said Billy munching on a mouthful of blossoms.

"Oh, please don't eat up my new home, Billy!" cried Hedley in dismay.

"No, no, just having a taste. I'll keep it well trimmed for you, Hedley. That's what I do best you know."

"Alright." said Hedley. " You keep my new home tidy and I'll keep the bugs off your favourite leaves."

"Sounds like a good idea, Hedley. I'm going to enjoy having you living here. It's nice to make new friends. Speaking of friends, where is Marvin?"

"Here," squeaked the mouse, "under the rhubarb. This is a great place to settle down."

"Just make sure that Aunt Jane doesn't see you." warned Billy. "She gets very upset when mice get in the house."

"Don't worry" said Marvin. "Screeching humans upset me, too!"

"Talking of humans," said Hedley, "I had better be getting back to the cart. James may be wondering where I am. Coming, Marvin?"

"If you don't mind," said Marvin, "I would prefer to go exploring."

Grandfather was looking out of the kitchen window. "Do you see that!" said Grandfather. "Hedley has found a friend already."

"Bless my soul!" said Aunt Jane. "Hedley is a very special hedgehog. I can see why you wanted to bring him with you, James. Well, he is certainly welcome here, as long as he stays outside."

"I'm sure Hedley has had enough of shoeboxes. I wouldn't be surprised if he has made a home under the hawthorn hedge." said Grandfather.

"Look, Robert!" laughed James. "Hedley has made friends with Billy the goat. Come out and meet him."

"Well, Jane my dear. I'm sure Hedley will be a great help in the garden. By next spring, you may have a few more spiny visitors. It would be nice for Hedley to have friends of his own kind. But then, I suppose we'll just have to wait and see. I'm quite sure that this is just the beginning of Hedley's adventures in Somerset!"